The Magic of Misty Nook

Kitty Kat Rescue: Little Frank's Story

Christine Skippins

Copyright © 2023 Christine Skippins

christineskippinsauthor@gmail.com

Christineskippinsauthor.com

FIRST EDITION

Kitty Kat Rescue, run by Chief Elf Dawn and her helpers, is one of a group of Misty Nook animal centres. They care for the animals that stay there with kindness and magic. This is the story of how the Kitty Kat Elves helped a little cat called Frank.

Frank had been in trouble more than he deserved.

Little Frank arrived at Kitty Kat Rescue in a bit of a state. At just four months old, he was a handsome young lad, with large, pointed ears and characterful white markings placed on his shiny black coat. All topped off with some very impressive long white whiskers.

Frank was adventurous and sporty by nature, and loved Zoomies time, especially when it involved climbing, chasing, bouncing, and pouncing.

"Hi everyone, my name is Frank, and my favourite pastime is exploring. All the nooks have to be inspected."

"I am independent and impetuous. I jump first and worry about the consequences afterward. My adventures have got me into much mischief in my brief life. We cats have nine lives, but

1

I have used two of mine, the first when I fell into a tall butt of water, nearly drowning, and then breaking my elbow. I don't want to waste anymore, so I need to be careful."

Kitty Kat Rescue Elves knew Frank needed help. They could see that he had something wrong with his back leg when they arrived at his home. The Elves persuaded his owner to let them take him to the animal centre with them and give him the help that he needed.

Once he was in their care, they rushed him to see the Kitty Kat centre vet.

Frank was frightened, but he remembered they were trying to help him.

"My leg was so painful. I was grateful to the Elves. I felt sad that I didn't know what was happening to me."

"The kind vet said that she was going to help me, then started by putting a sharp thing called a needle into my skin. I remember meowing in protest. I needed to let her know she had just caused me more pain."

The vet examined him whilst the Elves stroked and talked to Frank. They explained the sharp prick came from a needle that delivered an injection. This would relieve the pain and make him sleepy. The vet could then take a special picture of his leg.

They established Frank had broken the bone on his elbow on his back leg. It needed to be supported with a splint and a bright green bandage to help it heal.

Frank's eyes dull as he recalls the pain.

"I fell into a deep sleep on the vet's table that day. When I awoke, they had set my basket down in a nice, quiet, warm nook. I still felt strange and unsteady. My mouth was so dry. Dribble was soaking my white furry bib. Weariness engulfed my small body as I snuggled into the soft, warm blankets in my basket. My eyes tried so hard to stay open, but my body had other ideas. The more I tried to fight it, the more I yawned, and I yawned, and I yawned, until I gave in and dozed off again, visiting a land of wonderful dreams and the most amazing adventures. Until the alien, numbing, and snoozy sensations crashing through my small furry body from the injections subsided."

"I remember little about those first few days at Kitty Kat Rescue, but I do remember the warmth and snugness of my nook. I was grateful that the awful pain had dulled."

The Elves always post stories about the animals in their care on Kitty Kat Rescue's social media.

Their kind supporters send them many lovely get-well wishes and contributions towards the cost of their treatment.

"The Elves sat and read all of my get-well wishes to me. The kindness shown touched me. My heart burst with joy and warmed me inside and out."

"I am a sunny-side-up kind of cat. I felt happy and grateful to be getting my elbow fixed. The Elves knew I wasn't afraid. I had never felt a sense of calm like the one I experienced at Kitty Kat Rescue. Perhaps it was the magic. Perhaps it was just being surrounded by so much love and care. I will never know. I will always be grateful."

Frank went to the vet many times. The next visit followed a few days later.

"This time I knew what to expect. The Elves had prepared me for my visit to the vet. I sat tall in my cage. The pain in my leg had been relieved by the medication. I was keen to check out the veterinary area that I was in."

"With the next injection, I was ready for the prick of the needle. I slumped into another deep, adventure-filled sleep so that the vet could do what she needed and see if the damaged bones in my leg were healing."

"When I woke up again, I was woozy. My initial reaction was to stand up, but my bad leg was bound up in yet another large awkward green bandage. My other three legs wobbled. I crashed down into my cage's soft blanket."

Frank was quick to understand that it was much more comfortable to lie down with his small body arranged around the stiff new bandage on his poorly leg.

After taking the medication, he couldn't sit up, but he was chatting. He caught the eye and the ears of anyone who passed by his nook. When hands reached into the cage to stroke him, he bumped his head against them and provided purrs that an idling tractor would be proud of. He delivered head bumps with all the force that he could muster from his laying position. The Elves could not resist rewarding him with a wonderful, gentle cuddle.

Frank reflects.

"The Elves were so kind. I think they understood I was trying hard to be brave, and not let my discomfort colour my mood. I was worried about this thing called a splint on my leg. As the days passed, both it and the bulky bandage that held it in place became uncomfortable. My paw was sore, and my leg was sweaty. This, along with constant confinement to a cage, was testing my good humour - and my patience."

"Cage rest continued for what seemed like an eternity. I spent my time in a variety of sitting, lying, or half-sitting and half-lying positions. I tried to get comfortable. The Elves were going about their chores, and I chatted with them. They allowed me out for cuddles, special delicious food, drinks, or if I needed the toilet. Let me tell you, using a litter tray, even a special one, with a plaster cast on your leg is difficult for a cat. Especially one that likes to be clean at all times."

By this point in his recovery, Frank was visiting the vet every week. She liked him and praised him for his patience. He was resting and being very good-natured with her, and the Elves, despite his discomfort.

Frank's whiskers twitch, and he rolls his eyes in amusement.

"I mean, like I had a choice. If you are always in a cage, you cannot do anything else."

But he still purred to thank her for her care as she removed him from his confinement and rewarded his good humour with a cuddle.

The familiar pattern of injection followed by dream-filled sleep and a fresh crisp bandage emerged as the vet checked on the progress of his bones fusing back together. She and the Elves were happy with his progress.

Frank felt better, and his mood brightened.

"It may be my impetuous nature that had resulted in me being here, but as I felt better, it resurfaced. I wanted to join the Elves and did not stop to give any consideration to how I could stand unsupported on my poorly leg. Whatever it takes to make it work, I will do."

"I am a very smart little cat, and as my recovery continued, they moved me to a cage with more headroom that filled my cosy nook. Me being me meant I was quick to solve how to sit up, as well as a work-in-progress signature hobble that supported my bandaged leg. It was difficult to place my legs on the floor without getting hurt. I needed more time to recover.

The Elves were keen that Frank was very careful with his poorly leg, so they discouraged any hobbling.

Blessed with a smart brain, oodles of charm, and handsome good looks, Frank had the Purrfect catitude package. He used this to his great advantage, winning the hearts of everyone around him. His days with the Elves settled into a routine, and they all became a family.

He learned that a sad face, with big saucer eyes, encouraged the swift arrival of some treats from the Elves to cheer him up.

A chatty face with wide bright "please talk to me" eyes always resulted in a pleasant chat with his Elf friends. If he tilts his head, it could be super engaging.

Head bumps to the cage attract a head and neck stroke.

Talking of strokes, Frank thought,

"I am looking forward to some tummy strokes once my leg is better. I am rather proud of my silky soft white tummy and intend to show it off."

Frank had a lot of time to think as he recovered from his accident. He reflected often on what he had learned during his Kitty Kat Rescue stay.

"A big lesson learned is that vets are good. They work very hard to keep us fit and healthy, and fix us when we get ourselves into trouble. I get to see much bigger and braver cats than me, hissing and shouting at the Elves as they're brought past my nook to go to the vet's room. All that stress just seems so unnecessary, and a waste of energy. They need to follow my example and learn the lesson that I did. Vets and Elves are kind and caring. Maybe they aren't as smart as me."

The vet was happy to sign Frank off. With his leg fixed, if he was careful and did not go climbing trees, she felt he could move into the larger nooks. She could allow him to move around and play.

Frank was joyous at the news.

"I was ready for a game with a ball or feather. My new, bigger nook had access to some space outside. Through its door was a magical wonderland of autumn smells. A fresh nip in the air, soft golden light, and crisp red, yellow, and gold leaves to chase around and rustle in. It was fun to play again."

"That's how I met Sparkle, a beautiful young cat who was staying next to me. She was sad because her sister, Fizz, had just died, and the tip of her sleek black tail was just poking through the bars. She sat heartbroken in her nook. Me being me, I could not resist giving it a gentle tap with my striking white paw. At first, Sparkle reacted with a twitch. I took it as an invitation to tap it again. Each time I tapped, she twitched it more, and that was how we became friends."

"Having Sparkle as a friend brought a whole new warm glow to my life. I loved showing her my toys and pranced around my nook like a cartoon cat that had just helped himself to the finest steak. I had never had a friend before, and I liked Sparkle. She was the most beautiful cat that I had ever seen. I just loved playing and chatting with her."

The Elves spotted the budding friendship, and they gave Sparkle and Frank the chance to bond. They tried out sharing a nook. Frank was very macho. He just wanted to play and cuddle and bounce and pounce. At first, Sparkle found him overwhelming, but she grew to adore him, and just loved him even more for his awkward attempts to impress her. The Elves promised to find them a home where they could be together forever.

"Thank you, Kitty Kat Rescue. You are magic and have changed our lives and the lives of all the cats that stay in your nooks. With love from Frank and Sparkle."

Montage of pictures of Little Frank and Sparkle's stay at Kitty Kat Rescue.

Afterword

I would like to thank Dawn and the Team at Kitty Kat Rescue for allowing me to write about this special little guy. I will donate 50% of all Royalties to the charity as Little Frank's and Sparkle's legacy.

07957 324322

kittykatrescue1@hotmail.com

https://www.facebook.com/kittykatrescueandrehoming/

If you enjoyed Little Franks Story please consider leaving a review.

Your feedback helps me provide the best reading experience for readers. It would mean a lot to me if you would follow this link to share your thoughts on this book.

https:// christineskippinsauthor.com/ReviewLittleFrank

You can sign up for my newsletter at
www.christineskippinsauthor.com/FreeBook

Email me directly at
ChristineSkippinsAuthor@gmail.com

Or visit my website
www.christineskippinsauthor.com

Thank you

Printed in Poland
by Amazon Fulfillment
Poland Sp. z o.o., Wrocław

17608736R00016